To **Mason**
The star of the story!
From

Mason was VERY excited as it was the day before Christmas Eve, and everyone was rushing around getting everything ready for the celebrations ahead.

4

Cards had been posted,
twinkly lights had been put
up and Christmas trees
had been decorated.

5

There was also another
special event taking
place on this busy day -
    the Christmas baking competition!
Tasty goodies of all kinds would be judged,
    with the VERY BEST declared the overall winner!

This year's very important judge was Santa Claus, who had been flown in by Rudolph on his sleigh.

7

All the bakers
were busy making
their goodies.

There were mince pies,
yule logs, festive cakes,
scrumptious puddings
and of course
Christmas cookies.

8

Mason, who was on Santa's nice list and had been specially invited to watch the baking competition, noticed that one of the contestants, a little gingerbread boy, was crying. "Hello, what's the matter?" Mason asked kindly.

The gingerbread boy sobbed to Mason that he was ready to decorate his gingerbread cookies but that all his icing, raisins and chocolate buttons had gone MISSING!

"Don't worry," Mason gently told the gingerbread boy. "I will help you to look for them."

The gingerbread boy jumped for joy, then pointed to the clock on the wall. They didn't have much time as Santa would soon start the judging.

Mason began to look for clues - perhaps one of the other bakers had hidden the decorations!

They looked in Big Bear's back pocket.

They looked under Happy Hare's hat.

They even looked behind Eager Elf's ears, but the decorations were nowhere to be found!

Then, just as they were about to give up, clever Mason noticed a little trail of icing sugar on the floor leading to the back door and it had some very strange-looking footprints in it!

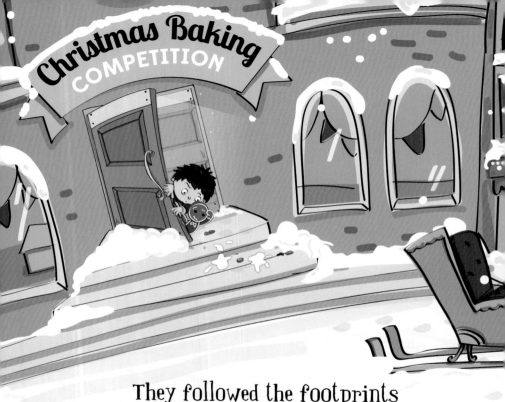

They followed the footprints
and as they stepped outside they saw
some icing splats and blobs, and a few
raisins that had been dropped.

"Can you hear that?" Mason asked the gingerbread boy.

There was a loud crunching followed by an even louder munching sound coming from Santa's sleigh.

15

Chewing on a crunchy carrot while singing some rather out of tune Christmas songs was Rudolph - and he was busily decorating reindeer shaped cookies with the missing decorations!

"Rudolph, what are you doing?" exclaimed Mason. "The gingerbread boy needs those decorations!"

Rudolph explained that he just wanted to borrow them so he could enter the competition himself.

"I have a brilliant idea!" said Mason. "You can help us decorate the cookies."

They all rushed back into the hall to get started as time was running out.

19

Icing, chocolate buttons and raisins flew everywhere as one by one the tasty gingerbread cookies were decorated and finished in the nick of time.

The three looked on nervously as Santa came to the table to inspect all the entries.

20

Then to their complete surprise he announced that Mason, Rudolph and the gingerbread boy were the winners... and to Rudolph's dismay the first prize was a trip in Santa's sleigh!

The end

COLOUR
ME IN